# A Palette of Whispers

*Poems from the Heart of an Artist*

# A Palette of Whispers

*Poems from the Heart of an Artist*

Priya Das

VerseWave™
Crafting Your Story

**ISBN: 978-81-981815-2-7**



First Edition



*Published by*
**VerseWave: Crafting Your Story**
Belghoria, Kolkata 700056
Website: www.versewavepublishing.com

# Content

# About the Author

Priya Das is a skilled graphic designer, currently working at 5 Core, with a deep passion for art and creativity. She studied at St. Augustine Day School and pursued her college education at the prestigious Government College of Art and Craft, Calcutta, specializing in Modelling and Sculptures. Priya's artistic journey is marked by numerous achievements, including winning twice during her college years, judging Durga Puja events for ABP News and Srijan, and securing 2nd position in a Canva graphic design competition.

## Preface

In a world filled with noise and distraction, the life of an artist can feel like a lonely journey. *A Palette of Whispers* captures this experience—a heartfelt reflection on the highs and lows of hustling as a young artist.

Within these pages, you'll find poems that express the hope, resilience, and raw beauty found in both triumphs and struggles. Each piece is a gentle reminder that art is not just a product but a journey, painted with our dreams and experiences.

I invite you to let these whispers resonate with your own journey. Welcome to *A Palette of Whispers*, where art, ambition, and the human spirit intertwine.

# Chasing the Dawn

In the quiet hours before the sun,
I sketch my dreams, where shadows run.
Colors blend in a canvas bright,
A world unfolds in the morning light.
With every stroke, I fight my doubt,
Hoping the world will hear my shout.
Brush in hand, I seize the day,
In this hustle, I find my way.
Though the road is tough and the path is long,
In art, I find where I belong.
With passion fierce, I'm set to soar,
This is my life; I crave nothing more.

## Canvas of Struggles

The blank canvas stares, silent and white,
A reflection of battles I must fight.
Doubt whispers softly, “Will you succeed?”
But I push back, fueled by the need.
With colors of courage, I paint my fears,
Transforming the doubts into vibrant tears.
Every brushstroke tells a story untold,
Of dreams on the line, of hopes turned bold.
I’ll rise from the ashes, no fear in my heart,
For in every struggle, I find my art.
In the chaos, I flourish, and in pain, I thrive,
Through the storm of ambition, I feel alive.

# The Artist's Soliloquy

In the stillness of night, when the world is asleep,
I delve into colors, my secrets to keep.
With every flick of the brush, I set my soul free,
Expressing my thoughts through the art inside me.
A symphony of hues, a dance of despair,
In silence, I speak to the world with care.
For the canvas listens, with patience and grace,
It holds my whispers, my dreams in its embrace.
Though the world may judge, I remain true,
In the depths of creation, I find something new.
An artist's journey is rarely a straight line,
Yet through each twist and turn, my spirit will
shine.

# Echoes of Inspiration

In crowded rooms where silence speaks,
I find inspiration in the voices of the weak.
Every story shared, every tear that falls,
Becomes the rhythm that fuels my calls.
From city streets to hidden trails,
I gather fragments of life's vast tales.
With every heartbeat, I weave the threads,
Creating a tapestry where no one dreads.
In the chaos, I see beauty unfold,
In the mundane, there's magic untold.
With passion ablaze, I rise to create,
An artist's mission is to elevate.

## Sketches of Resilience

With pencils in hand, I carve my fate,
Each sketch a testament to dreams I create.
Lines may falter, but I press on through,
In every mistake, I find something new.
The world is a canvas, wild and vast,
I embrace my journey, forgetting the past.
With every misstep, I learn to adapt,
Building my vision, no longer entrapped.
Resilience blooms in the face of the fight,
An artist's heart glows, ignited by light.
Through trials and triumphs, I stand up tall,
For in the struggle, I find my all

# The Hustler's Anthem

I rise with the sun, ready to grind,
In a world of chaos, I seek and find.
With dreams in my pocket and hope in my veins,
I hustle through doubts, dance in the rains.
Each rejection I face is a step toward my goal,
Fueling the fire that ignites my soul.
I'm not just an artist; I'm a warrior at heart,
Fighting through shadows, embracing the art.
With each beat of the drum, I carve out my place,
In the competitive noise, I find my own space.
This anthem of hustle, I sing loud and clear,
For in this wild journey, I have no fear.

# Chasing Shadows

In crowded galleries, I weave through the throng,
Chasing shadows where I feel I belong.
Every glance, every whisper, a spark in my chest,
Yet the weight of the world puts my dreams to the test.
I blend in the colors, a vibrant disguise,
But inside, I'm longing to rise and surprise.
With passion as my compass, I won't lose my way,
In the shadows, I find light, come what may.
For every brushstroke, a piece of my heart,
In this endless chase, I'll never depart.
With hope as my guide, I'll fight for my name,
In a world of shadows, I'll carve out my fame.

## Heart on My Sleeve

With my heart on my sleeve and dreams in my gaze,
I step into the world, ready to blaze.
The canvas before me, a mirror of soul,
In colors and strokes, I find my control.
Every piece I create, a reflection of me,
In each hue, my essence is free.
Through struggles and triumphs, I lay it all bare,
For the artist within me knows no despair.
I'll paint my truth, let my spirit ignite,
For in this wild dance, I find my light.
With every creation, my heart beats strong,
In the rhythm of passion, I've always belonged.

## Fragments of Dreams

Scattered like leaves in the autumn breeze,
My dreams dance wildly, searching for ease.
With a brush as my guide, I gather each piece,
Creating a world where doubts find release.
In the fragments of life, I find my design,
A mosaic of moments, uniquely mine.
From whispers of hope to colors that sing,
In the chaos of creation, my spirit takes wing.
Each struggle I face becomes part of the whole,
An artist's journey, a quest for the soul.
In every heartbeat, I paint my own fate,
For the dreams I pursue will never abate.

## Waves of Emotion

In the tides of emotion, I ride the waves,
Capturing moments that the heart craves.
With every brushstroke, I channel my fears,
Transforming my pain into vibrant tears.
The ocean of creativity flows through my veins,
In the ebb and the flow, I break my chains.
From the depths of sorrow to peaks of delight,
I paint my truth, bold and bright.
For in this journey, I’m learning to swim,
Embracing the light where shadows grow dim.
An artist's soul, fierce and unbound,
In the waves of emotion, my voice is found.

## The Price of Passion

With passion ignited, I dive into the fray,
Every moment I cherish, every struggle I slay.
But the price of this dream is heavy to bear,
As I navigate waters of doubt and despair.
In the marketplace hustle, I fight for my space,
In a world full of art, I yearn to leave a trace.
Every rejection, a lesson, each failure a guide,
Through the storms of ambition, I refuse to hide.
For my heart beats louder than fears in my head,
In the quest for my passion, I'll never tread dead.
In the tapestry of life, I weave my own thread,
For the price of this passion is one I'll not dread.

# Embers of Creativity

In the quiet corners of a bustling cafe,
I let my imagination run wild and sway.
With coffee in hand and thoughts like fire,
I sketch my dreams, fueled by desire.
Inspiration sparks from the people I see,
Each life a story, each glance a key.
As I transform moments into art on my page,
The embers of creativity burn bright with rage.
Through laughter and tears, my brush takes flight,
In the dance of expression, I find my light.
With every creation, my spirit ignites,
In this world of wonder, I'll reach new heights.

## The Road Less Traveled

With every step on this uncertain road,
I carry my heart, my dreams, my load.
In the face of the crowd, I stand alone,
An artist's journey is uniquely my own.
The whispers of doubt may cloud my sight,
But I'll forge ahead, ready to fight.
For the path is winding, filled with despair,
Yet in every challenge, I find the rare.
In the art of persistence, I carve my own way,
A testament to dreams that refuse to decay.
The road less traveled is where I belong,
In the heart of the hustle, I find my song.

## Mosaic of Life

In pieces of life, I gather my art,
Creating a mosaic from the depths of my heart.
Every fragment a story, a memory bright,
Each color a chapter, a spark in the night.
From laughter to sorrow, I blend them with care,
Building a canvas that's uniquely rare.
In the chaos of creation, I find my release,
Transforming the broken into something that's peace.
For the art of my life is a journey unbound,
In the richness of struggle, my voice is found.
A tapestry woven with threads of my soul,
In this beautiful chaos, I finally feel whole.

## Glimmers of Hope

In a world of ambition where dreams can fade,  
I cling to the glimmers that hope has made.  
Through the shadows of doubt, I search for the light,  
Finding strength in the journey, my heart burning bright.  
Every setback a lesson, every scar a guide,  
In the face of the storm, I'll never subside.  
With every brushstroke, I paint my own fate,  
In the hustle of life, I embrace what I create.  
For hope is the fuel that ignites my desire,  
In the fires of passion, I rise even higher.  
As an artist, I'll forge through the darkest of nights,  
With glimmers of hope, I'll reach new heights.

## Whispers of the Heart

In the stillness of night, when the world is asleep,
I listen to whispers that my heart keeps.
Each stroke of the brush tells stories untold,
Of dreams and desires, of hopes made bold.
With every creation, I share a piece,
Of my soul and my journey, seeking release.
For art is my language, my truth in the dark,
In the silence, I find the spark.
With each moment captured, I let go of pain,
In the whispers of the heart, I find my gain.
Through the rhythm of creation, I reclaim my voice,
In the world of art, I finally rejoice.

# Threads of Connection

In the threads of connection, I find my way,
Through the stories of others, I paint my stay.
Every person I meet leaves a mark on my soul,
In the tapestry of life, we all play a role.
From shared laughter to tears softly shed,
Each interaction is a path I tread.
In the art of togetherness, I find my muse,
With every brushstroke, I refuse to lose.
For the power of connection fuels my heart's song,
In the beauty of community, I've found where I belong.
As an artist, I weave these threads with care,
Creating a masterpiece that we all can share.

## Rising from Ashes

In the ashes of dreams that once seemed so bright,
I rise with the dawn, ready to fight.
For every setback, I gather my strength,
In the depths of despair, I find my length.
With courage ignited, I forge my own way,
Turning struggles to triumphs, come what may.
In the art of resilience, I find my true voice,
In the chaos of life, I make my own choice.
With every creation, I rise from the flame,
For the heart of an artist is wild and untamed.
Through the trials of life, I'll stand strong and tall,
For in every setback, I learn to enthrall.

# Symphony of Dreams

In the symphony of dreams, I play my part,
With notes of ambition that flow from the heart.
Each brushstroke a melody, each color a tune,
In the orchestra of life, I'll find my own rune.
With the rhythm of passion, I dance through the day,
Creating a masterpiece in my own unique way.
Though the world may be loud, I'll find my own sound,
In the harmony of hustle, my spirit is found.
For the artist within me knows how to sing,
In the symphony of dreams, I embrace everything.
With hope as my conductor, I'll rise above,
Creating a world that echoes with love.

## Veins of Inspiration

In the veins of inspiration, I feel the pulse,
As creativity flows, a vibrant convulse.
From city lights to the whispering trees,
Every moment I capture, every breeze.
In the chaos of life, I find my muse,
In the smallest of details, I refuse to lose.
For the heart of an artist beats wild and free,
With every creation, I set my spirit to flee.
Through the colors of life, I'll weave my design,
In the tapestry of dreams, my soul will shine.
In the veins of inspiration, I'll never run dry,
For the heart of a hustler will always fly high.

## Reflections of Tomorrow

In the mirror of today, I see my dreams,
Shattered yet whole, bursting at the seams.
With every reflection, I gather my grace,
In the journey of hustle, I find my place.
Though the world may shift, and tides may turn,
In the flames of ambition, my passion will burn.
With eyes set on horizons yet to unfold,
I'll navigate paths, both gentle and bold.
For the future is bright, a canvas to fill,
In the reflections of tomorrow, I find my will.
With courage as my armor, I step into the light,
An artist of life, ready to ignite.

# Journey of the Heart

With each step I take on this winding road,
I carry my heart, my dreams, my load.
In the hustle of life, I dance with the beat,
Finding joy in the struggle, making my retreat.
For the artist within me knows no bounds,
In the journey of the heart, true freedom is found.
With every creation, I express my soul,
In the tapestry of life, I find my role.
Though the world may challenge, I'll rise above,
In the journey of the heart, I'll spread my love.
For every moment lived is a brushstroke divine,
In the art of existence, I'll forever shine.

# Fires of Ambition

In the fires of ambition, I kindle my flame,
With dreams in my heart and a hunger untamed.
Each day I awaken, ready to fight,
In the world of creation, I find my light.
Through struggles and victories, I carve my own path,
In the heat of the moment, I unleash my wrath.
For the artist within me knows how to strive,
In the flames of passion, I truly feel alive.
With every setback, I rise even higher,
Fueled by the dreams that never expire.
In the fires of ambition, I'll blaze my own way,
For the heart of an artist is fierce and will sway.

# Whirlwind of Colors

In the whirlwind of colors, I find my release,
A cacophony of hues, a moment of peace.
With every splash, I let go of the pain,
Transforming my chaos into art that remains.
From the depths of my heart, I conjure each shade,
In the palette of life, I'm never afraid.
For the artist within me knows how to play,
In the dance of creation, I find my way.
Through the whirlwinds of life, I'll paint my own truth,
In the colors of passion, I'll rediscover youth.
With every stroke, I'll craft my own tale,
In the whirlwind of colors, I shall prevail.

# Infinite Possibilities

In the realm of creation, where dreams intertwine,
I explore infinite possibilities, bold and divine.
With each brushstroke, I open new doors,
In the canvas of life, my spirit soars.
Through the laughter and tears, I find my own grace,
In the heart of the hustle, I carve my own space.
For the artist within me knows how to grow,
In the depths of uncertainty, my passions will flow.
With every creation, I break through the chains,
In the tapestry of life, I dance in the rains.
For the journey ahead is mine to define,
In the world of possibilities, my heart will shine.

## Echoes of Purpose

In a world full of voices louder than mine,
I listen closely for my echo, faint yet divine.
Through chaos and chatter, I carve my own way,
Holding fast to my purpose, come what may.
With every stroke, my intentions grow clear,
Even as doubt whispers faintly near.
For the artist's heart beats strong and true,
Through struggles endured and dreams pursued.
In the rhythm of creation, I find my peace,
Each echo of purpose, a sweet release.
With courage to guide me, I step toward light,
Turning whispers of doubt into art so bright.

# Silent Triumphs

Some victories speak without fanfare or praise,
Quietly earned through long, restless days.
In the solitude of my art, I find strength,
Each silent triumph stretched to its length.
Not every win is seen or known,
But in private growth, I've truly grown.
Through self-doubt's storms and late-night fires,
I fuel my path with unspoken desires.
For each canvas completed, each line refined,
Is a whisper of resilience, deeply aligned.
My triumphs may be silent, yet they ring clear,
For the artist's spirit holds each moment dear.

## Path of Colors

On a path painted with colors bold and bright,
I walk with dreams, guided by a flickering light.
With blues of calm and reds of fight,
My palette shifts through each day and night.
Every hue I mix is a piece of me,
My joys, my fears, my artistry.
Through shades of failure and strokes of gain,
My brush dances, releasing the strain.
For the colors I craft tell tales of my soul,
Each blending of shades, a step toward whole.
In the world of art, my heart finds its way,
A path painted anew with each dawn of day.

# Heartbeats in Ink

With each beat of my heart, I pour out ink,
Dipping into dreams without stopping to think.
My art is a rhythm, pulsing and true,
Capturing moments that life pushes through.
Each line a heartbeat, each word a sigh,
An artist's language beneath the sky.
For ink speaks what words may miss,
In the quiet hum of artistic bliss.
In struggles and hustle, I find my song,
Through pages filled, I journey along.
These heartbeats in ink are a piece of me,
Expressions of life, raw and free.

## Veils of Vision

Through veils of vision, I see my truth,
In colors of wisdom painted from youth.
The world beyond may seem distant and vast,
Yet my art reveals dreams from the past.
Each veil lifted, a secret shown,
In the layers of canvas, I find my own.
With hands that create, my heart becomes clear,
Breaking illusions I once held near.
For vision is born from struggle and grace,
In the journey of art, I find my place.
Through veils of vision, I paint my way,
Bringing hidden dreams into light each day.